The Wolf and the Seven Little Kids

A FAIRY TALE BY **Jacob & Wilhelm Grimm**

TRANSLATED FROM THE GERMAN BY **Anthea Bell**

ILLUSTRATED BY **Bernadette Watts**

North-South Books · New York · London

ONCE UPON A TIME there was an old mother goat who had seven little kids, and she loved them just as all mothers love their children.

One day she was going out to look for food, so she called all her seven little kids and told them, "Dear children, I'm going into the wood, so mind you watch out for the wolf! If he gets in here, he'll eat you up. The wicked creature often disguises himself, but you can recognize him easily by his hoarse voice and his black feet."

"We promise to be careful, dear Mother," said the seven little kids. "Don't worry!"

So Old Mother Goat bleated good-bye and went on her way.

Copyright © 1995 by Nord-Süd Verlag AG, Gossau Zürich, Switzerland
First published in Switzerland under the title *Der Wolf und die sieben jungen Geisslein*
English translation copyright © 1995 by North-South Books Inc.

First published in the United States, Great Britain, Canada,
Australia, and New Zealand in 1995 by North-South Books,
an imprint of Nord-Süd Verlag AG, Gossau Zürich, Switzerland.

Distributed in the United States by North-South Books Inc., New York.

Library of Congress Cataloging-in-Publication Data
Grimm, Jacob, 1785-1863.
[Wolf und die sieben Jungen Geisslein. English]
The wolf and the seven kids / a fairy tale by Jacob & Wilhelm Grimm;
translated from the German by Anthea Bell; illustrated by Bernadette Watts.
Summary: When six of her seven kids are swallowed by a wicked wolf,
Old Mother Goat devises a way to rescue them.
[1. Fairy tales.   2. Folklore—Germany.]   I. Grimm, Wilhelm, 1786-1859.
II. Bell, Anthea.   III. Watts, Bernadette, ill.   IV. Title.
PZ8.G882Wj   1995
398.2'0943045297358—dc20   95-2266

A CIP catalogue record for this book is available from The British Library.
ISBN 1-55858-445-5 (trade binding) 10 9 8 7 6 5 4 3 2 1
ISBN 1-55858-446-3 (library binding) 10 9 8 7 6 5 4 3 2 1
Printed in Belgium

Before long there was a knock at the door and the seven little kids heard someone say, "Open the door, dear children! Here's your mother back, with something for each of you."

But the seven little kids wouldn't open the door. "You're not our mother!" they called back. "Our mother has a soft, gentle voice, but yours is hoarse. You're the wolf!"

So the wolf went to the village store and bought a big piece of chalk.
He ate it, and it made his voice soft and gentle.

He came back and knocked on the door again. "Open the door, dear children! Here's your mother back, with something for each of you."

But one of the wolf's black feet was showing at the window, and when the seven little kids saw it, they said, "We won't open the door! Our mother's feet are all white, and yours aren't. You're the wolf!"

The wolf went to the baker and said, "I've hurt my paw! Please put some dough on it!" And when the baker had covered his paw with dough, the wolf went off to the miller and said, "Sprinkle some white flour on my paw."

The miller thought, "This wolf is planning to trick someone!" and refused.

But the wolf said, "If you don't do as I say, I'll eat you up!"

The miller was afraid, and sprinkled white flour on the wolf's paw.

Then the wicked wolf went back to the house for the third time, knocked on the door, and said, "Open the door, children! Your dear mother is home from the wood with something for each of you."

"Show us your feet first!" said the seven little kids. "Then we'll know whether you're our dear mother or not."

So the wolf held up his white paw to the window, and when the seven little kids saw it, they opened the door.

But it was the wolf who came in!

The seven little kids were scared, and tried to hide. One hid under the table, the second in the bed, the third under the stove, the fourth behind the curtain, the fifth in the dresser, the sixth under the wash-basin, and the seventh inside the grandfather clock.

But the wolf found them and gobbled up every single one of them, except the youngest, who was hiding inside the grandfather clock. The wolf didn't find him.

When the wolf had eaten the six little kids, he strolled out of the house, lay down in the meadow under a tree, and went to sleep.

A little later, Old Mother Goat came home. Oh, what a sight met her eyes!

The door of the house was wide open, the table, chairs, and benches had been knocked over, the washbasin was broken, the blankets and pillows were dragged off the bed. She looked for her children, but they were nowhere to be found. She called their names, one by one, but there was no answer.

At last, when she called to the youngest, a tiny voice replied, "Here I am, dear Mother, hiding in the grandfather clock."

She helped him out, and he told her the wolf had come and eaten all the others. Oh, how Old Mother Goat wept for her six little kids!

Then, in her sorrow, Old Mother Goat went out of the house with the youngest little kid running beside her. When she came to the meadow, she found the wolf sound asleep under a tree, and she saw something moving inside his full stomach.

"My goodness," she thought. "Can my poor children still be alive in there?"

Old Mother Goat ran home for scissors, a needle, and thread. Then she began cutting open the wicked wolf's stomach. No sooner had she made the first cut than one of the little kids put its head out, and as she went on cutting, all six jumped out one by one. They were all alive and had come to no harm, because in his greed the wicked wolf had swallowed them whole.

How happy they were! They hugged their dear mother and hopped about merrily.

But Old Mother Goat said, "Go and find some big rocks, and we'll fill the wicked wolf's stomach with them while he lies there asleep."

So the seven little kids hurried off to collect rocks, and put as many as they could in the wolf's stomach. Then Old Mother Goat quickly sewed it up again.

When the wolf finally woke up, he was thirsty, so he decided to go to
the well for a drink.

But as he began to move about, the rocks in his stomach rattled and clattered. "What's that thumping and bumping inside me?" cried the wolf. "I ate six little kids, but it feels like rocks."

And when the wolf came to the well and leaned over to drink, the heavy rocks dragged him in and he was drowned.

When the seven little kids saw the wolf disappear, they ran up, shouting, "The wolf is dead! The wolf is dead!" and Old Mother Goat and her seven little kids danced around the well for joy.